Waltham Forest Libraries   L

Please return this item by the last date stamped. The loan may be renewed unless required by another customer.

06/2019		

Need to renew your books?
http://www.walthamforest.gov.uk/libraries or
Dial 0333 370 4700 for Callpoint – our 24/7 automated telephone renewal line. You will need your library card number and your PIN. If you do not know your PIN, contact your local library.

D1495128

'The Llama's Pyjamas'
An original concept by Jenny Jinks
© Jenny Jinks

Illustrated by Addy Rivera Sonda

Published by MAVERICK ARTS PUBLISHING LTD
Studio 3A, City Business Centre, 6 Brighton Road,
Horsham, West Sussex, RH13 5BB
© Maverick Arts Publishing Limited May 2019
+44 (0)1403 256941

A CIP catalogue record for this book is available at the British Library.

ISBN 978-1-84886-443-6

www.maverickbooks.co.uk

Blue

This book is rated as: Blue Band (Guided Reading)
This story is decodable at Letters and Sounds Phase 4/5.

The Llama's Pyjamas

by Jenny Jinks

illustrated by Addy Rivera Sonda

Larry was fed up.

"I am hot!" he said.

"My wool is too thick."

"Go for a swim," said Terry.

Larry swam in the pool.

Larry's wool got wetter and wetter, and bigger and bigger. But he was still hot.

"Sit under the tree," said Terry.

Larry sat under the tree.

But the twigs stuck in his wool.

And he was still hot.

"I can help," said Edna.

SNIP!

SNIP!

SNIP!

"You look odd," said all the llamas.

But now Larry was not hot.

He was not wet. He did not itch.

"I like my short hair," he said.

But when the sun went down,

Larry got cold. He began to shiver.

"I miss my wool," he said.

Larry was fed up.

But Terry had a plan.

"Put your wool back on," said Terry.

Larry got his wool and put it back on.

But the wool did not stick.

"Brrrrrr," Larry said.

He was still cold.

"I can help," said Edna.

She took Larry's wool.

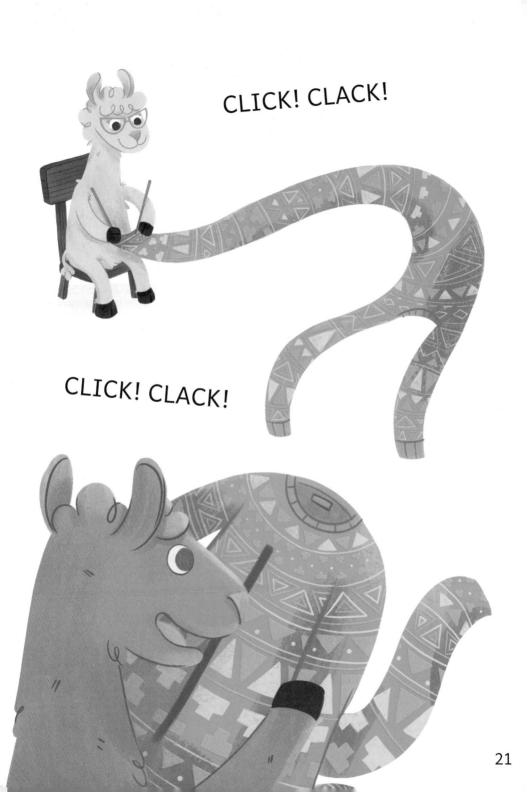

CLICK! CLACK!

CLICK! CLACK!

21

"What are they?" said all the llamas.

"You look odd."

But now Larry was not cold.

"I like my pyjamas!" he said.

Now Larry ran in the sun and swam in the pool.

And when it got cold, he was snug in his pyjamas.

"I wish we were like Larry," all the llamas said.

"Can you help us too?" the llamas
said to Edna.

"Yes!" said Edna.

SNIP! SNIP!

CLICK! CLACK!

Now all the llamas had short hair.

And they all had a...

...LLAMA PYJAMA PARTY!

Quiz

1. What is Larry?
a) A llama
b) A dog
c) A cat

2. What happens when Larry goes for a swim?
a) He gets cold
b) His wool gets bigger and bigger
c) He gets hot

3. "I can help," said _____.
a) Terry
b) Ben
c) Edna

4. Why does Larry feel cold?

a) Because the sun went down

b) Because his wool is sticky

c) Because Terry has pyjamas

5. And when it got cold, he was _____ in his pyjamas.

a) Hot

b) Snug

c) Cold

Book Bands for Guided Reading

The Institute of Education book banding system is a scale of colours that reflects the various levels of reading difficulty. The bands are assigned by taking into account the content, the language style, the layout and phonics. Word, phrase and sentence level work is also taken into consideration.

Maverick Early Readers are a bright, attractive range of books covering the pink to white bands. All of these books have been book banded for guided reading to the industry standard and edited by a leading educational consultant.

Pink
Red
Yellow
Blue
Green
Orange
Turquoise
Purple
Gold
White

To view the whole Maverick Readers scheme, visit our website at www.maverickearlyreaders.com

Or scan the QR code above to view our scheme instantly!

Quiz Answers: 1a, 2b, 3c, 4a, 5b